Awesome Animals
Rhymes & Recipes

Tracy Going

PENGUIN BOOKS

PENGUIN BOOKS

Published by the Penguin Group

Penguin Books (South Africa) (Pty) Ltd, 24 Sturdee Avenue, Rosebank, Johannesburg 2196, South Africa
Penguin Group (USA) Inc, 375 Hudson Street, New York, New York 10014, USA
Penguin Group (Canada), 90 Eglinton Avenue East, Suite 700, Toronto, Ontario, Canada M4P 2Y3 (a division of Pearson Penguin Canada Inc)
Penguin Books Ltd, 80 Strand, London WC2R 0RL, England
Penguin Ireland, 25 St Stephen's Green, Dublin 2, Ireland (a division of Penguin Books Ltd)
Penguin Group (Australia), 250 Camberwell Road, Camberwell, Victoria 3124, Australia (a division of Pearson Australia Group Pty Ltd)
Penguin Books India Pvt Ltd, 11 Community Centre, Panchsheel Park, New Delhi – 110 017, India
Penguin Group (NZ), 67 Apollo Drive, Mairangi Bay, Auckland 1310, New Zealand (a division of Pearson New Zealand Ltd)

Penguin Books (South Africa) (Pty) Ltd, Registered Offices: 24 Sturdee Avenue, Rosebank, Johannesburg 2196, South Africa

www.penguinbooks.co.za

First published by Penguin Books (South Africa) (Pty) Ltd 2011
Copyright © Tracy Going 2011

ISBN 978-0-14-352752-7

Photographs by Charles Heiman
Designed and Typeset by Susan Heiman
Illustrations by Kym Surmon
Printed and Bound by 1010 Printing International

Foreword

Awesome Animals – Rhymes & Recipes is the second in what I anticipate will be a series of cookbooks. I hope that you will enjoy this journey through the intriguing world of awesome animals as much as I have. I also hope that the animals come alive for you as much as they have for me through many months of interesting research. The more I have learned about each animal, the more I have come to realise how magnificent animals are with their individual personalities and their little quirks, just as interesting as all us different human beings!

This book, however, would not have been possible without the support of my patient husband and my enthusiastic children who are always keeping an eye out for new recipes and ideas. Their love of cooking and reading and their fascination with wild animals has certainly kept me encouraged and determined to finish this book.

I would also like to thank the rest of the team, in particular the delightfully calm chef Stacey Janse van Rensburg, for patiently and wholeheartedly trying out all my recipes and making them look and taste fantastic. We spent many hours in the kitchen, formulating, testing and photographing these recipes. It would be remiss of me not to mention that the time wouldn't have been quite the same without the assistance of the always-smiling Eloise Seekoei. Thanks to the two of you! I think the recipes are great – and I hope you think so too!

The book would also not have been quite as splendid without Kym's wonderful illustrations. Kym Surmon, your passion and fervour is apparent and I think all will agree that it has been successfully transferred onto these pages. Thanks for sharing your awesome artistic flair with us.

To my talented friends Sue and Charles Heiman – you are absolute stars. Charles, much appreciation for the hours you spent behind the camera capturing these wonderful culinary images! Sue, once again thanks for the days spent labouring over our work and putting it all together in this fabulous book.

I would also like to thank Reneé Naudé at Penguin Books for her enthusiasm and support, as well as Amelia de Vaal for her creative input. Thanks to the two of you: Your collective influence has been essential to the synergy of this project.

While on the subject of synergy, we constantly need to remind ourselves that life is not always about taking but also about giving and sharing. It is for this reason, once again, that a percentage of the proceeds will be donated to Child Welfare South Africa, an organisation that provides an essential service to those little ones who have been abused, neglected or abandoned. Thank you for your generosity and support of this worthy cause.

Until next time, may you spend many pleasurable hours reading – and do enjoy the sheer pleasure of whipping up amazing meals for all your family and friends!

Bon appétit

Tracy

Contents

A is for amazing, awesome animals found all around,
The Creator's best art that abounds above the ground.
From the vast Americas, across Africa and over Asia;
From the pole of Antarctica to the plains of Australia.

These splendid beasts exist from before our ancestors –
Some are meek and mild, others are vicious predators.
Some are short and fat, others so very tall and slender –
All so magnificent in their naturalness and splendour!

They live to be free and just take every day as it comes
And make time to have fun in the sun with their chums.
That life is about dancing, movement and stylish grace –
And that each of us has our own special, unique place!

They show us that we humans have so much to learn:
To be kind every day, and never our friends to spurn.
To live beside each other and just accept who we are;
Know that we don't always have to be a leading star!

That life is about patience, the point will finally come
For us to do our deeds and duties that have to be done.
To know we're to be courageous, brave and also bold
And do the right thing, not only when we're told.

That once the fight is over and there is no more threat,
We should then smile, forgive and always forget.
Make the world a better place as we do not live apart –
And live life as the animals do, so clever and so smart.

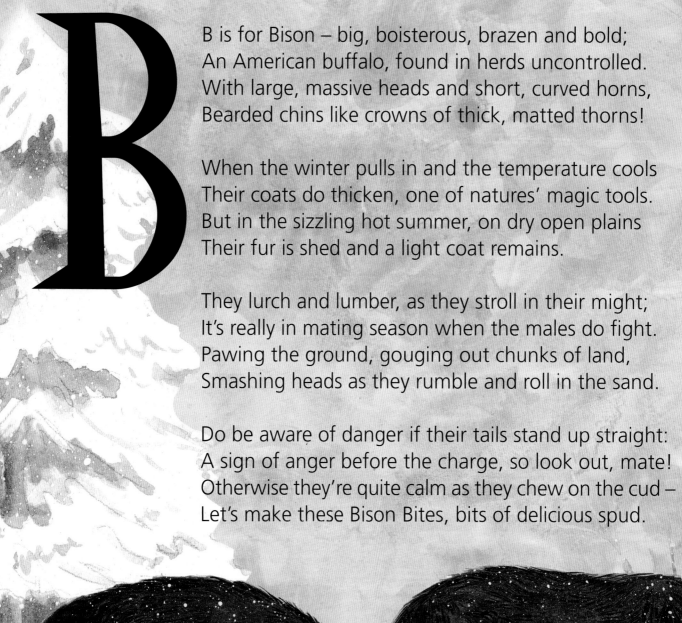

B is for Bison – big, boisterous, brazen and bold;
An American buffalo, found in herds uncontrolled.
With large, massive heads and short, curved horns,
Bearded chins like crowns of thick, matted thorns!

When the winter pulls in and the temperature cools
Their coats do thicken, one of natures' magic tools.
But in the sizzling hot summer, on dry open plains
Their fur is shed and a light coat remains.

They lurch and lumber, as they stroll in their might;
It's really in mating season when the males do fight.
Pawing the ground, gouging out chunks of land,
Smashing heads as they rumble and roll in the sand.

Do be aware of danger if their tails stand up straight:
A sign of anger before the charge, so look out, mate!
Otherwise they're quite calm as they chew on the cud –
Let's make these Bison Bites, bits of delicious spud.

Bison Bites

These blistering hot potato Bison Bites will have you lumbering with energy for the rest of the day.

YOU NEED:

4 baking potatoes
30 ml flour
5 ml fresh or dried rosemary
1 clove garlic, crushed
Olive oil
Salt and pepper

TOOLS:
Baking tray
Knife
Spatula
Oven gloves

HOW TO MAKE IT:

- Preheat the oven to 200°C or 400°F
- Cut each potato in half, then cut each half lengthways into 3 big chips
- Put the potato chips into a bowl
- Toss over the flour and add rosemary, garlic, salt and pepper
- Toss well
- Drizzle a little olive oil onto the baking tray
- Bake in the middle of the oven for 20 minutes
- Turn the potatoes and cook for another 20 minutes until crispy and golden

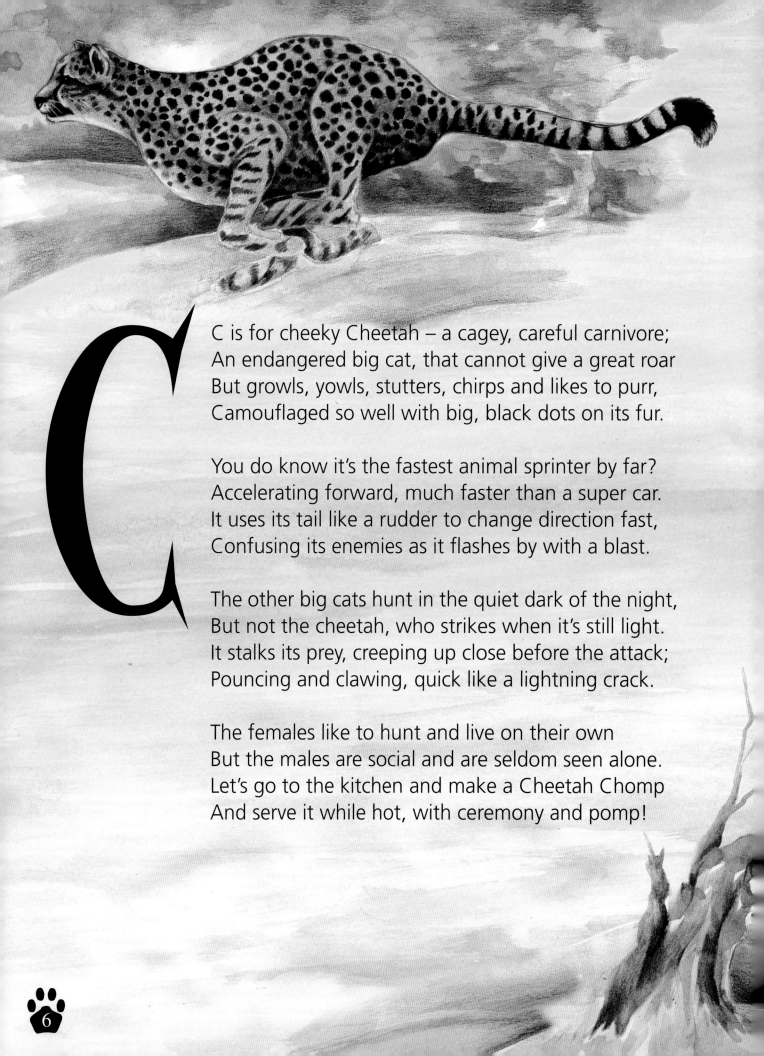

C is for cheeky Cheetah – a cagey, careful carnivore;
An endangered big cat, that cannot give a great roar
But growls, yowls, stutters, chirps and likes to purr,
Camouflaged so well with big, black dots on its fur.

You do know it's the fastest animal sprinter by far?
Accelerating forward, much faster than a super car.
It uses its tail like a rudder to change direction fast,
Confusing its enemies as it flashes by with a blast.

The other big cats hunt in the quiet dark of the night,
But not the cheetah, who strikes when it's still light.
It stalks its prey, creeping up close before the attack;
Pouncing and clawing, quick like a lightning crack.

The females like to hunt and live on their own
But the males are social and are seldom seen alone.
Let's go to the kitchen and make a Cheetah Chomp
And serve it while hot, with ceremony and pomp!

Cheetah Chomp

These cheerful Cheetah Chomps will have your friends and family pouncing about with lightning speed.

YOU NEED:

250 ml flour
10 ml baking powder
250 ml grated cheddar cheese
125 ml milk
1 extra-large egg
Pinch of salt

TOOLS:

Sieve
Mixing bowl
Spoon
Measuring cups
Muffin tins
Oven gloves

HOW TO MAKE IT:

- Preheat the oven to 180°C or 350°F
- Grease the muffin tins with a bit of butter or cooking spray
- Sift the flour and baking powder together
- Add the rest of the ingredients and mix well
- Spoon the mixture into the muffin tins, filling the hollow just over halfway
- Bake for 15 minutes

D is for the dazzling Dinosaur, so definitely dead –
Land-dwelling reptiles, with a world-wide spread.
Having disappeared about sixty million years ago –
Whew, what an incredibly long time ago, my bro!

Splendid beasts, roving the earth rigid and erect –
But I'm really quite glad we didn't have to connect!
Some walked on two legs and some walked on four;
Many were quite tall, with others closer to the floor.

Some had several horns, or even a high crest;
Some were protected with an armour-plated breast.
They used to be thought of as stupid and slow;
Now it's believed they were bright and in the know.

Either way, they must have been a terrifying sight,
These wondrous beasts filled with powerful might.
Let's whip up this easy and tasty Dinosaur Drizzle
And give our daily salad some much-needed sizzle!

Dinosaur Drizzle

This delectable Dinosaur Drizzle dressing
will definitely add dazzle to any fresh salad.

YOU NEED:

100 ml balsamic vinegar
200 ml olive oil
5 ml Dijon mustard
10 ml honey
1 clove garlic, crushed

HOW TO MAKE IT:

- Mix all the ingredients together
- Pour into a nice small jug
- This can be kept in the fridge until needed

TOOLS:

Fork
Measuring cups
Small mixing bowl
Small jug

E is for the extremely exotic and enormous Emu:
A big Australian bird, that rhymes with kangaroo;
With shaggy, soft brown feathers, it's unable to fly
But with its fast, steady trot it's so agile and spry.

Don't get a fright if you hear a large, loud boom:
It's how they converse in their outdoor chat-room.
And on scorching hot days they pant to keep cool,
Or swim, play and splash in any open water pool.

She lays thick-shelled green eggs in a small batch,
And he's the one that covers them until they hatch.
And protects them, loves them, just sorts them out
Until they're big enough to be out and roundabout.

With pebbles and stones, it's strange what they eat,
But grasshoppers and crickets are a really big treat.
A gathering of Emus is commonly known as a mob –
How about Emu Entrees? Let's get on with the job!

Emu Entrees

These exotic Emu Entrees will entice and encourage any healthy appetite.

YOU NEED:

4 eggs
50 ml Narwhal Naise (or any favourite mayonnaise)
30 ml pecan nuts, chopped
10 ml fresh parsley
Salt and pepper
1 packet leafy green salad
50 ml Dinosaur Drizzle (or any favourite dressing)

TOOLS:

Small pot
Spoon
Knife
Cutting board
Measuring spoons

HOW TO MAKE IT:

- Put the eggs in a small pot and cover with cold water
- Place pot on the stove, and bring to the boil
- Boil for about 10 minutes, remove from heat and drain water
- While the eggs are cooling, divide the salad between 4 plates
- Drizzle the salad with Dinosaur salad dressing
- Once eggs have cooled, shell them
- Slice the eggs in half lengthways
- Pop two egg halves onto the plated leafy salad
- Add a spoon of mayonnaise to each egg
- Sprinkle with pecan nuts and parsley
- Add salt and pepper to taste and serve

F is for the fast, fit, ferocious Fossa with feisty flair,
Wearing a golden brown coat and a wide open stare;
Short, powerful legs and sharp, retractable claws;
It has scissor-like teeth and violent, and vicious jaws.

Found deep in the forests on the isle of Madagascar,
A wonderful place off the south-east coast of Africa,
You might believe the fossa is seen only out at night –
It's just because they like to keep out of human sight.

This remarkable predator is really a mean little beast,
A carnivore that eats all, as part of its fine daily feast:
From snakes to fishes and birds, it's quite a schemer!
Not troubled to hunt or hound even the largest lemur.

A distant cousin to the mongoose, a fact that is true!
Although it looks like a cat and behaves like one too.
It scampers and leaps from one branch to even three –
Oh, these Fossa Friandises! So fantastic, you will see!

Fossa Friandises

These Fossa Friandises are fantastically fluffy and fine –
and will also have you flying from tree to tree!

YOU NEED:

15 g flour
175 g desiccated coconut
90 g sugar
1 egg white

HOW TO MAKE IT:

- Preheat the oven to 180°C or 350°F
- Beat the sugar and egg white until the mixture is fluffy
- Add the coconut and flour
- Mix well with a spoon
- Take a heaped tablespoon of the mix and shape into a pyramid
- Place the pyramids onto a baking tray
- Pop into the oven for about 15 minutes

TOOLS:

Mixing bowl
Electric beater
Spoon
Tablespoon
Scale
Baking tray

G is for gruff Gorilla, a great, goofy, gentle giant;
Somewhat shy and friendly, not known as defiant.
It lives on the ground and rarely climbs into trees
And is closely related to humans by a few degrees.

Spot the bulging forehead, tiny ears and bright eyes;
Known for its intelligence and for being very wise.
With long legs, bulky body and a big, broad chest,
In a browny-black coat, it's fairly funkily dressed.

With a grunt, growl and barking cough it does stalk
Down on its knuckles, doing a strange knuckle walk,
Beating at its chest with a loud and deafening 'ha!',
An echoing sound filling the rainforests of Africa.

Being in a forest must be like living in a restaurant:
Munching mostly on leaves from the nearest plant.
Put on the oven and let's make these Gorilla Grills –
A scrumptious, succulent snack, without any frills!

Gorilla Grills

These great Gorilla Grills will have everyone
grunting, groaning and growling with gusto!

YOU NEED:

1 pack big black mushrooms
2 cloves garlic, crushed
5 ml fresh thyme
125 g feta cheese, crumbled
Salt and pepper

TOOLS:
Paper towel
Baking tray
Knife
Spatula
Oven gloves

HOW TO MAKE IT:

- Turn on the grill
- Wipe the black mushrooms clean with the paper towel
- Trim the mushroom stalks if needed
- Place mushrooms on a baking tray with the stalks facing up
- Sprinkle with garlic, thyme and salt
- Crumble the feta cheese over the mushrooms
- Pop under the grill and cook until they are ready
- Grind some black pepper over for serving (optional)

H is for the handsome Hedgehog, hasty and haughty,
With spines on its back, it's so very cute and naughty.
Check out the large pointed ears and very sharp snout
As it scuttles and scampers in the scrub roundabout.

Hedgehogs are mainly spotted hurtling on the ground,
Squealing, grunting or making a soft, snuffling sound.
But they can also swim and can clamber up very tall trees,
And roll into a ball, then drop, not hurting knees.

As solitary animals they prefer to be left on their own,
Minding their business in their own hedgehog zone.
To protect themselves, they roll up into a firm little ball
And will rather run from attack than have a nice squall.

On the hunt, they use great skill to hear and to smell,
Not relying on eyesight, that is neither good nor swell,
And feed on slimy snails, green frogs and yucky toads –
The hearty Hedgehog Hiccups will definitely feed loads!

Hedgehog Hiccups

No one will be haunted by hunger after eating
these hearty and healthy Hedgehog Hiccups!

YOU NEED:

1 tin asparagus
60 g butter
4 tablespoons flour
1 teaspoon salt
350 ml milk
6 medium eggs, separated
125 ml cheddar cheese, grated
Cooking spray

TOOLS:
Tin opener
Knife
2 mixing bowls
Beater
Small pot
Wooden spoon
4 ramekins

HOW TO MAKE IT:

- Preheat the oven to 200°C or 400°F
- Prepare each ramekin with cooking spray
- Drain the tin of asparagus, squeeze out all the liquid
- Cut the asparagus into small pieces
- In a bowl, stir together the egg yolks
- In another bowl, beat the egg whites until very stiff
- In a pot, over low heat, mix the butter and flour and slowly add the milk
- Stir until the sauce thickens
- Remove from heat
- Season with salt
- Add the asparagus
- Slowly add the hot mixture to the egg yolks while stirring
- Fold in the stiff egg white mixture
- Add the grated cheese and mix carefully
- Spoon into ramekins
- Bake for about 20 minutes until golden and well risen

I is for the impish Ibex, so impressive and incredible;
So amazingly agile with such wicked mountain skill!
Found in Eurasia, as well as in North and East Africa,
When you spot one, allow yourself to shout 'Eureka!'

You'll only find them high on steep mountain slopes,
Scurrying and scaling the cliffs of nature's tightropes.
Quite a feat, standing on hind legs, stretching at roots,
Leaves and lichen, tall shrubs and fresh tender shoots.

The ibex is celebrated as a great, wild mountain goat.
It's the males that have a bushy beard on the throat.
They also have those big, magnificent gnarled horns –
Superior and more spectacular than even a unicorn's!

Watch out for fights as they shove to see who is best:
Threatening, they lock horns, putting skill to the test.
Quite aggressive, these goats with a head for heights –
Now for the Ibex Ice, some rather delectable delights!

Ibex Ice

This incredible Ibex Ice is the ultimate indulgence after a good meal.

TOOLS:
Small pot
Measuring cups
Wooden spoon

YOU NEED:

40 g treacle sugar
15 ml golden syrup
40 g butter
100 ml fresh cream
5 ml vanilla extract

1 tub of your favourite vanilla ice-cream

HOW TO MAKE IT:

- Melt sugar, syrup and butter in a pot to make the butterscotch sauce
- Bring to the boil and keep stirring for a few minutes
- Remove from the heat and stir in the cream and the vanilla
- Allow to cool
- Serve on top of your favourite ice-cream

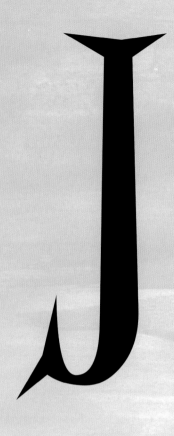

J is for the jaunty, jumping and quite jazzy Jaguar:
A fine feline found over much of Central America,
From Mexico to the Argentine pampas and plains;
The third largest cat, after a tiger and lion, it claims.

The dense rainforest is its preferred habitat,
Camouflaged in rosettes, a bold, black paint splat!
With underbelly, throat and lower flanks so white,
These compact beasts are full of power and might.

A stalk-and-ambush guy that doesn't like to chase,
It gives an almighty paw swipe to an enemy's face.
It does have a roar, a sound like an ongoing cough,
And many a grunt to show it's so rough and tough.

This spotted cat is active between dusk and dawn:
Alone, stalking what is left of the Creator's lawn.
Unfortunately, today jaguars are seen less and less –
This Jaguar Juice will show off your kitchen finesse!

Jaguar Juice

This Jaguar Juice is just what you need to jazz up any table – and just so you know: it will be ready in a jiffy!

YOU NEED:

2 large pineapples
3 large carrots

HOW TO MAKE IT:

- Skin the pineapples and cut into big chunks
- Peel the carrots and cut into big slices
- Pop into a juice maker
- Serve in tall glasses with lots of ice

TOOLS:

Knife
Cutting board
Juice maker
Tall glasses

K is for a kind Koala, a klutzy kind of knockout kid –
To the east and south of Australia they are often hid.
Just for your information, it is not some type of bear:
It's a marsupial, like its cousin the kangaroo, I swear.

Found in eucalyptus trees, holding its standard pose,
With large, fluffy ears and a big black leathery nose.
Thick, woolly fur protects it in the heat and the cold
And they sleep about sixteen hours a day, I'm told!

When born, they're so small, the size of a jelly bean,
Called a 'joey' when they first come onto the scene.
Warmly tucked in mom's pouch, all safe and sound –
Only at six months do they start moving out around.

Do you know they have their very own fingerprints?
And because of what they eat, they smell of mints?
Usually quite silent, the males have a very loud call –
Let's make the Koala Krunch and have a ball!

Koala Krunch

This crispy Koala Krunch is perfect for your daily lunch.

YOU NEED:

2 tin lentils
1 small onion
20 sundried tomatoes
Fresh basil leaves
60 ml Dinosaur Drizzle (or any salad dressing)
Salt and pepper

4 fresh crispy rolls
Extra olive oil for drizzling

TOOLS:

Tin opener
Knife
Chopping board
Small bowl

HOW TO MAKE IT:

- Open the tins of lentils, wash and drain
- Put the sundried tomatoes in a bowl of hot water to rehydrate for about 5 minutes, then cut into fine slices
- Chop the onion very finely
- Break the basil leaves into bits
- Mix the lentils, onion, sundried tomato, basil and Dinosaur Drizzle
- Add salt and pepper to taste
- Cut the crispy rolls in half
- Top each half with some of the Koala Krush and drizzle with extra olive oil

L is for the lurking and lavish Lynx, living in a lair,
Seldom seen around and sadly now rather rare.
In North America, Europe and Asia they're dotted;
Some are striped or freckled and others are spotted.

With thick fur for warmth in the chilly winter glow,
And padded paws for those living deep in the snow;
Fabulous with a short neck and the flared facial ruff
And black tufts on the ears, such splendorous stuff!

They don't really utilize their feeble sense of smell,
But this is what makes them at night-hunting excel,
As with such style they track with a listen and a look,
Stalking their prey in every forest cranny and nook.

They hunt on the ground, scaling trees out of sight,
And only venture about in the deep dark of night.
Only way to find them is to search for their tracks –
Let's rustle up the Lynx Lite, which will serve stacks.

Lynx Lite

The Lynx Lite will have you leaping and loping with loads of energy!

YOU NEED:

3 cups water, boiling
4 tea bags
60 ml honey
3 cups apple juice
Mint for garnish and flavour

HOW TO MAKE IT:

- Pour the hot water into a jug and steep the tea bags for 5 minutes
- Strain out the bags
- Stir in the honey and apple juice
- Mix until dissolved
- Chill in the fridge
- Serve on ice and with sprigs of mint

TOOLS:

Measuring cup
Mixing jug
Spoon
Glasses and pitcher (to serve)

M is for magical, mysterious and mighty Moose,
Found in the north of America, just hanging loose.
With a heavy body and spindly legs, quite a deer!
And those huge antlers, oh, my! Such funky gear!

Males drop the antlers at the end of mating season –
And don't believe that it is for no rhyme or reason:
All to save energy when winter the cold does bring,
And a brand new set will grow back in the spring!

Males fight each other to see who makes the grade,
Otherwise only aggressive when attacked or afraid.
But don't get caught between a calf and its mother:
Then you're in for a chase and a fright, my brother!

Do you know they dive under the water very deep?
And swim for ages, just enjoying the water sweep?
Ok! So their hollow hair does help them stay afloat –
Let the Moose Mousse just slide down your throat.

Moose Mousse

This magical Moose Mousse is a must for those
who need a melt-in-the-mouth treat after a meal.

TOOLS:
Beater
2 mixing bowls
Spoon

YOU NEED:

150 g milk chocolate, broken up
75 ml butter
3 extra-large eggs, separated
1 egg white
125 ml cream, stiffly beaten

HOW TO MAKE IT:

🦌 Melt chocolate in the microwave and remove
🦌 Add the butter and stir until melted
🦌 Add the eggs yolks one by one, beating well each time
🦌 Beat the egg whites (with clean beaters) until stiff
🦌 Fold the egg white into the chocolate mixture
🦌 Spoon into glasses and chill in the fridge for a few hours
🦌 Serve with whipped cream

N is for natty Narwhal, a noble, nautical nomad,
In a blue-grey and white suit, magnificently clad.
Its long, twisted tooth is the first thing you'll see:
A glorious creature, the unicorn of the Arctic sea.

They hang out together in a gang known as a pod,
Snacking the day away on shrimp, squid and cod.
They don't catch food using their tusk as a spear
But suck their meal in as it goes by past and near.

In winter they live deep under the solid pack ice;
In summer it's a frolic in shallow waters, so nice.
With a gentle roll and sway, no need to be quick,
Making a deafening whistle, trill, squeal or click.

Killer whales and Greenland sharks they do fear,
And thanks to man, they're almost gone, oh dear.
And climate change is not helping them so much –
This Narwhal Naise should be a very nice touch!

Narwhal Naise

Narwhal Naise is a mayonnaise which will add a nice, nifty twist to any nosh.

YOU NEED:

2 egg yolks
200 ml sunflower oil
10 ml Dijon mustard
20 ml lemon juice
20 ml white vinegar
5 ml salt

TOOLS:

Electric beater
Mixing jug
Spoon

HOW TO MAKE IT:

- Place the egg yolks, mustard, lemon juice, vinegar and the salt into a mixing jug
- Beat briefly
- While still beating, add the oil drop by drop until you have a thick delicious mayonnaise

O is for the odd Okapi, so original and outrageous,
With a camouflage coat that is quite advantageous.
You might look and think it's a zebra, half and half,
But it's actually a rather fine-looking forest giraffe!

Only to be found deep in the heart of Africa, though,
In a place called the Democratic Republic of Congo.
Down in the rainforest, where it's so incredibly wet,
Its velvety suit doubles as a raincoat, with no sweat.

With a horse-like head, thick neck and black muzzle,
And horizontal stripes on the legs, it's quite a puzzle.
A sticky, blue tongue is for picking leaves out about;
Also fine for washing eyelids and ears inside or out.

As a shy and solitary animal they only mix to breed,
Circling each other with a sniff and a lick it's agreed.
With large ears to warn, if there's any leopard about –
Yes, it's Okapi Oodles, you'll shout without doubt!

Okapi Oodles

This Okapi Oodles is loaded with goodness –
and is obviously an outstanding option for an opulent meal!

YOU NEED:

2 tins chickpeas
1 onion, chopped
1 tin tomatoes, chopped
30 ml olive oil
250 ml vegetable stock
Salt and pepper
1 bunch fresh coriander

TOOLS:
Tin opener
Colander
Wooden spoon
Medium pot
Cutting board

HOW TO MAKE IT:

- Open the tins of chickpeas, wash and drain
- Open the tin of tomatoes
- Heat the oil in a pot and add the onions.
  Cook slowly until they become soft
- Add the tin of tomatoes and simmer for 10 minutes
- Add the chickpeas
- Add the vegetable stock
- Add some salt and pepper
- Add half the coriander, chopped
- Bring to the boil and allow to
  simmer for about 15 minutes
- Serve in a bowl or with some
  rice and garnish with the
  extra coriander

P is for precious giant Panda, so perfectly padded;
Poised and polished, I think it could be added!
Found down in the grand bamboo forests of China;
Known as a big bear cat, not much could be finer!

Notice the black eyes, ears and belt upon its throat:
A daring contrast to its brilliant white, woolly coat.
Which probably assists to camouflage in the snow?
That is what scientists think but don't really know.

The diet is simple: it's ninety-nine percent bamboo,
But fishes and eggs, yams and bananas will also do.
Sitting or lying as they munch away the long hours,
Gnawing with teeth, seven times larger than ours!

Clawing at trees, they mark their own special space,
Taking shelter in tree hollows – what a perfect place!
They don't hibernate, but do move to a warmer land –
Let's whip up these Panda Puffs, a dessert so grand!

Panda Puffs

These pears on a Panda Puff are a powerful way to end off a perfect meal.

YOU NEED:

1 tin pear halves, drained
1 roll puff pastry
10 ml nutmeg
Cooking spray

1 tub vanilla ice-cream

TOOLS:
Baking tray
Knife
Tin opener
Spatula
Oven gloves

HOW TO MAKE IT:

- Heat the oven to 180°C or 350°F
- Prepare a baking tray using cooking spray
- Cut out circles of pastry a bit bigger than a pear half
- Place the circles of pastry onto the greased baking tray
- Place a pear half flat side up on each pastry circle
- Sprinkle with a little nutmeg
- Place in the oven and bake for about 20 minutes
- Serve with a good dollop of your favourite ice-cream

Q is for the quirky, quiet, quick, quizzical Quoll:
An Australian marsupial, what a cute little soul!
There are quite a few different kinds and species,
Of which the terrific tiger quoll is one of these.

They live on the ground, flat on the forests floor,
In burrows and hollow logs, it's what they adore.
Only shimmying up tall trees, so as to be spared,
Hiding from eagles of which they're very scared.

Spot them at night, out hunting or just having fun,
So seldom seen basking out in the daylight or sun.
They're usually asleep, snuggled up tight in a den,
Popping out a pointed snout only now and again.

Notice the small white spots, even on the long tail,
With many sharp teeth, another interesting detail!
With a reddish brown, or even a darker coarse fur –
The Quoll Quesadillas will definitely cause a stir!

Quoll Quesadillas

These Quoll Quesadillas are so quick to make and will have you quaking and quivering with delight.

YOU NEED:

4 tortilla wraps
4 spinach leaves, finely sliced
100 g grated mozzarella cheese
5 ml oregano
5 ml thyme
3 sliced peppadews (optional, as they can be spicy)
Salt and pepper
Cooking spray

TOOLS:

Baking tray
Knife
Cutting board
Spatula
Oven gloves

HOW TO MAKE IT:

- Heat the oven to 200°C or 400°F
- Prepare the baking tray with cooking spray
- Place 2 tortilla wraps onto a preparation surface
- Top each tortilla wrap with some spinach
- Season with salt, pepper and fresh herbs
- Sprinkle with peppadews
- Top with grated mozzarella cheese, but stay away from the edges
- Cover with another tortilla wrap
- Place onto the baking tray and bake for about 15 minutes until crispy and golden

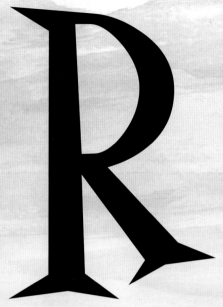

R is for the roving, radiant, rather racy Raccoon:
An intelligent mammal, definitely not a buffoon.
But they're really known for their big, black eyes,
Looking so bright and cheerful and ever so wise!

They can't really see much colour or see very far,
But can see green in sight, which is a bit bizarre!
They do hear all sorts of different kinds of sound –
Even earthworms moving deep under the ground.

They don't like being out and about in open land,
Rather hiding in forests, near water and wet sand.
Most of the food is found in rivers, using the paw,
Swiping at crayfish and frogs, which must be sore.

Hoping to score fish down in the deep water dregs,
And also hunt mice and raid nests for any eggs.
As omnivores, they eat all different things and bits –
Let's go to the kitchen and make the Raccoon Ritz!

Raccoon Ritz

This Raccoon Ritz with nuts and seeds is a rather rich relish.

YOU NEED:

2 ripe avocados
1 apple, finely chopped
½ stalk celery, thinly sliced
20 ml Narwhal Naise (or any favourite mayonnaise)
20 ml plain yoghurt
1 nectarine, thinly sliced
Seed and nut mix
1 packet leafy salad

HOW TO MAKE IT:

🐻 Mix together the apple, celery, Narwhal Naise and yoghurt
🐻 Cut the avocados in half lengthwise and take out the pip
🐻 Fill the centre of each half with the mix
🐻 Arrange on a bed of lettuce and decorate with the nectarine slices
🐻 Sprinkle with the seed and nut mix

TOOLS:

Knife
Cutting board
Spoon
Small mixing bowl

S is for the snazzy, sassy, somewhat stinky Skunk –
A cool, striped creature, oh yes, it's nature's punk!
Funky with the two white stripes on its black back,
With rather sharp claws used for digging its shack.

If really afraid, it will release its foul, smelly spray –
Such a vicious weapon, so please don't get in the way!
So horrible, it's even enough to ward off a big bear;
Luckily it usually just hisses or give a mean glare.

So! Not too many predators, as its spray does repel –
Aside from the horned owl with no sense of smell!
Usually found in dens lined in dry leaves and grass,
Found all over the Americas, they're not so sparse.

Eating frogs, lizards, even bees flapping fine wings,
Unafraid, as the fur is made to protect from all stings
But also dig in the grass for worms, bugs and slugs –
The sizzling Skunk Swirls should get you some hugs.

Skunk Swirls

These snazzy Skunk Swirls will be quite scrumptious and sumptuous.

YOU NEED:

1 butternut, sliced
30 ml honey
10 ml ground cinnamon
Olive oil

HOW TO MAKE IT:

- Heat the oven to 180°C or 350°F
- Slice the butternut into thin rings and remove any seeds
- Drizzle some olive oil onto the baking tray
- Place the butternut slices onto the tray and drizzle with the honey
- Sprinkle with cinnamon
- Pop into the oven and cook for 20 minutes
- Turn the slices over and cook for another 15 minutes

TOOLS:
Knife
Cutting board
Baking tray
Oven gloves

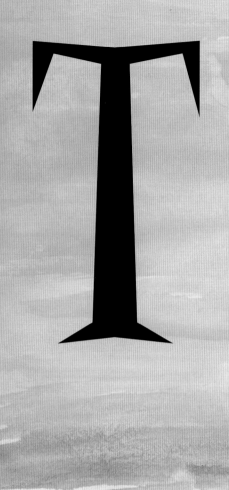

T is for the terrifying, tenacious and terrific Tiger –
Found in parts of Asia, Siberia, India and also China!
Bigger than the other cats lion, leopard or jaguar;
A solitary beast; beautiful, stealthy and muscular.

Apart from its massive bulk and awesome power,
It is awfully dangerous, and can a human devour!
But they prefer to eat deer, pigs, monkeys or birds
And bury the leftovers, in case they'll need thirds.

It is best known for its dark and vertical stripes,
From top to tail, even down its long sturdy pipes.
Do you know they also have stripes on their skin?
And they don't purr, not even from deep within?

Their very best is to swim in river waters so cool,
Leaping and loping around, just playing the fool!
Such a pity they are endangered and almost gone!
With the Tiger Tickles you'll feel big and strong.

Tiger Tickles

These tantalising Tiger Tickles will tempt even the toughest taste buds.

TOOLS:

Knife
Tin opener
Electric beater
Dessert glasses

YOU NEED:

2 tins mandarin oranges
1 tin granadilla pulp
250 ml fresh cream
1 tablespoon castor sugar

HOW TO MAKE IT:

- Layer the mandarin oranges into glasses
- Spread the granadilla pulp between the layers
- Leave in the fridge for a few hours before serving
- Whip the cream and castor sugar until thick and fluffy
- Serve the Tiger Tickles with a big dollop of cream

U is for the ultimate, ultra unbelievable Unicorn:
A mythical, magical creature known for its horn –
A fine, delicate spiral found on its splendid head,
Slicing the heavens like a mystical, silver thread.

A mighty mane streams towards its striking rear;
Cloven hooves akin to those of an untamed deer.
Amazing from its crown all down its long length,
This creature, a startling sight of super strength.

Ferociously fierce, it fills the air with great allure
And symbolises all that is honest, good and pure.
Only to be tamed by a young maid, pure and fair,
This mystical beast of feisty flash and fine flare.

Many believe that unicorns once really did exist.
Wouldn't that be a tale with an interesting twist?
Let's go and make a Unicorn Utopia for our sup –
Everyone will be screaming, 'Hey what's up?'

Unicorn Utopia

This ultra-healthy Unicorn Utopia is an unforgettable dish and is so unbelievably easy to make!

YOU NEED:

125 g uncooked twisted pasta
1 tin corn
1 handful watercress, coarsely chopped
50 g feta cheese, crumbled
50 g sundried tomatoes
3 tablespoons olive oil

TOOLS:
Big pot
Colander
Spoon
Knife
Chopping board
Bowl

HOW TO MAKE IT:

- Cook the pasta as per the instructions on the packet
- Drain the pasta and allow to cool
- Soak the sundried tomatoes in a bowl of hot water for 5 minutes to re-hydrate and then cut into thin slices
- Add the sundried tomatoes, corn, watercress and feta cheese to the cold pasta
- Add the olive oil, salt and pepper

V is for the very verbal, vibey and vigilant Vicuna:
A camel found in the mountains of South America,
With large, round eyes and a dense cinnamon coat –
Look out for the pompon on its long, supple throat.

Always on alert, it flees at the first whiff of danger,
Running like the wind every time it sees a stranger.
With a loud warning call, a shrill, shrieking whistle,
So different from its hum, like a soft pennywhistle.

The hooves give sure footing on high, rocky slopes;
Walking on its soles, no stumble or fall one hopes!
As it flexes its toes and grips at loose gravel stone,
Always with its family, never on its own, all alone.

Some say the vicuna's wool is the best to be found:
Softer, lighter and warmer than any others around;
Great for the mountain climate, often wet and cold.
This Vicuna Vichyssoise is delicious, so I'm told!

Vicuna Vichyssoise

This Vicuna Vichyssoise soup will be a veritable feast,
giving you much-needed vitality on a very hot day.

YOU NEED:

6 leeks, washed and sliced
3 potatoes, peeled and cubed
1 vegetable stock cube
500 ml water
250 ml fresh cream
30 ml olive oil
Pinch nutmeg
Salt and pepper

TOOLS:

Pot
Peeler
Knife
Cutting board
Blender
Spoon

HOW TO MAKE IT:

- Fry the leeks in the oil on medium heat until soft
- Add the cubed potatoes, water, and vegetable stock cube
- Bring to the boil and allow to simmer until
  the potatoes are soft
- When cooked, remove from the stove and blend
- Add salt, pepper and a pinch of nutmeg
- If the soup mixture is too thick, add some water;
  if it is too thin, then pop the pot back
  onto the stove and boil further
- Once the soup has cooled, add the cream
- Serve at room temperature

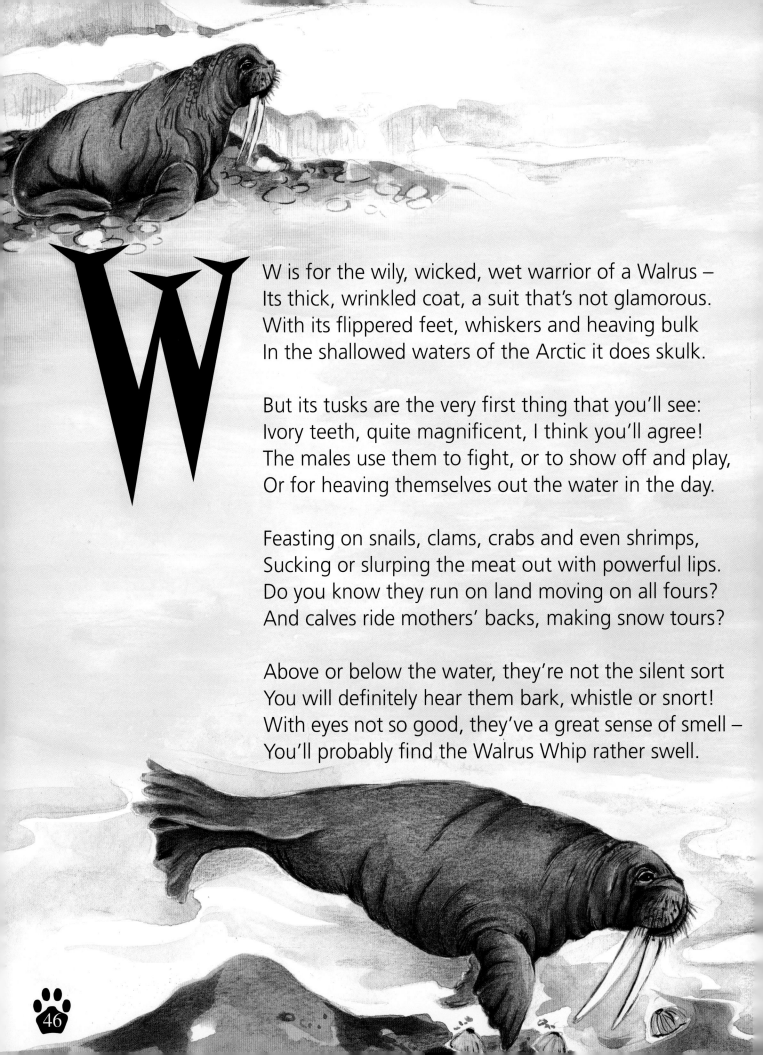

W is for the wily, wicked, wet warrior of a Walrus –
Its thick, wrinkled coat, a suit that's not glamorous.
With its flippered feet, whiskers and heaving bulk
In the shallowed waters of the Arctic it does skulk.

But its tusks are the very first thing that you'll see:
Ivory teeth, quite magnificent, I think you'll agree!
The males use them to fight, or to show off and play,
Or for heaving themselves out the water in the day.

Feasting on snails, clams, crabs and even shrimps,
Sucking or slurping the meat out with powerful lips.
Do you know they run on land moving on all fours?
And calves ride mothers' backs, making snow tours?

Above or below the water, they're not the silent sort
You will definitely hear them bark, whistle or snort!
With eyes not so good, they've a great sense of smell –
You'll probably find the Walrus Whip rather swell.

Walrus Whip

The Walrus Whip is a wondrous way to wet your whistle and won't leave you wanting.

TOOLS:
Blender
Glasses (for serving)

YOU NEED:

125 ml vanilla yoghurt
250 ml vanilla ice-cream
250 ml milk
4 large strawberries
125 ml tinned peaches

HOW TO MAKE IT:

- Wash the strawberries and remove any green leaves
- Blend all the ingredients together
- Chill and serve on ice

X is for the eXtra eXceptional order of Xenarthra,
Made up of the sloth, the anteater and armadillo.
Why put them together, these crazy little creatures?
Because of their unusual, yet very similar features.

All are known for being strange jointed mammals,
With extra moving parts, what interesting animals!
The skulls are extra long, a brain so small and thin,
A low body temp, saving energy till needed within!

They're found within the land of the vast Americas –
Go back eighty million years and find their replicas,
Existing from when earth was a very different place,
When rainforests did the big, whole world embrace.

Today we live in the tail end of the mighty Ice Age,
With melting polar caps in their last and final stage.
We need to do something, so global warming stops:
Let's save energy and make these Xenarthra Xops!

Xenarthra Xops

These Xenartha Xops are the extra X-factor
added to a meal, or just as an exciting snack.

YOU NEED:

500 g sweet potato, peeled and grated
250 ml flour
1 egg
80 g butter, melted
Salt
Oil
Boiling water

1 tub of your favourite dipping sauce

TOOLS:

Grater
Mixing bowl
Spoon
Deep frying pan
Paper towelling

HOW TO MAKE IT:

- Cover the grated sweet potato with hot water
  and stand for 15 minutes
- Drain well
- Mix the sweet potato, flour, egg and butter together
- Add salt as needed
- If the mixture is too stiff, add a little water; if it is
  too thin, add a little more flour
- Heat some oil in the frying pan
- Using a dessert spoon, drop the mixture
  spoon by spoon into the oil
- Fry on a medium heat until golden
- Drain on paper towelling
- Serve with your favourite
  ready-made dipping sauce

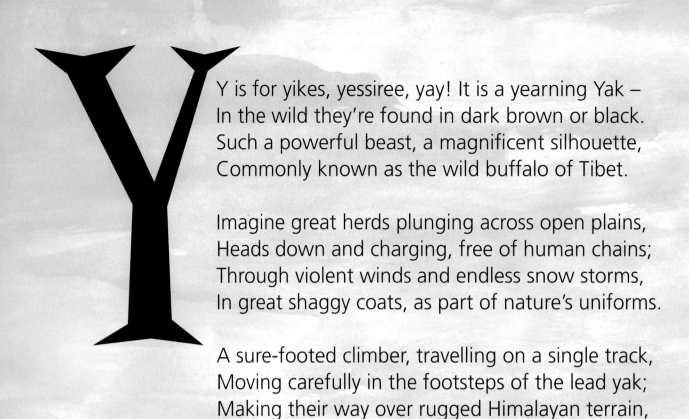

Y is for yikes, yessiree, yay! It is a yearning Yak –
In the wild they're found in dark brown or black.
Such a powerful beast, a magnificent silhouette,
Commonly known as the wild buffalo of Tibet.

Imagine great herds plunging across open plains,
Heads down and charging, free of human chains;
Through violent winds and endless snow storms,
In great shaggy coats, as part of nature's uniforms.

A sure-footed climber, travelling on a single track,
Moving carefully in the footsteps of the lead yak;
Making their way over rugged Himalayan terrain,
Looking for grass and lichen, but please no grain.

Known for their intelligence and great personality,
They can be rather shy, which is really a pity!
They live many years, some say more than twenty –
Let us make a big loaf of Yak Yum to feed plenty.

Yak Yum

This yummy Yak Yum should have you
yowling, yammering and yelping for more.

YOU NEED:

500 ml buttermilk
500 g self-raising flour
1 packet white onion soup
5 ml salt
Cooking spray

TOOLS:
Loaf tin
Mixing bowl
Spoon

HOW TO MAKE IT:

- Set the oven at 180°C or 350°F
- Spray the loaf tin with cooking spray
- Mix together the flour, salt, soup powder and buttermilk
- Pour the mixture into the prepared loaf tin
- Bake in the oven for one hour
- Serve warm with butter

Z is for the zealous Zebra of zany and zooty zest –
An African wild horse, so extremely well dressed.
White stripes on black? Or maybe black on white?
Either way, they're just a most magnificent sight.

Over vast plains they gallop, canter, trot or walk
With only one toe on a foot and a grand mohawk.
When cornered, they rear up as they kick and bite,
Or zigzag away as they try to avoid losing a fight.

Their big ears are used as part of their protection,
Swivelling around as they listen in any direction.
But when calm and friendly, their ears stand erect;
When afraid they're forward for danger to detect.

Did you know that zebras do stand as they sleep?
And whinny and bark with a high-pitched squeak?
Let us zip into the kitchen and make a Zebra Zing
As we end this book with a glass of blazing bling!

Zebra Zing

The zooty Zebra Zing is zesty and zany – and best of all: it is zippy to make!

TOOLS:
Chopping board
Knife
Blender
Tall glasses (for serving)

YOU NEED:

250 ml milk
250 ml vanilla yoghurt
250 ml vanilla ice-cream
4 apples
1 teaspoon cinnamon

HOW TO MAKE IT:

- Wash apples, peel, core and cut into bits
- Blend all the ingredients together
- Chill and serve in tall glasses with ice

Other Awesome Facts

Bison – As bison are so big, they don't have many predators; however, they are afraid of wolves. Bison also like to roll around in the mud and dust. This is part of their grooming, but it also helps to keep them cool and to keep insects away.

Cheetah – Cheetahs have an enlarged heart and lungs, as well as big nostrils to allow for a greater intake of oxygen. They might be able to reach 100 km/h (70 mph) in three seconds, but they can't run at these speeds for very long, as they get too tired. Cheetahs also can't retract their claws like the other big cats.

Dinosaur – The word 'dinosaur' means 'terrible lizard'. It is believed dinosaurs lived on earth for over 165 million years and mysteriously went extinct at a time when there was a lot of volcanic activity. Others believe dinosaurs might have been wiped out when a large comet struck the earth.

Emu – The emu is apparently unable to walk backwards. They have two sets of eyelids: one is used for blinking and the other is used to keep the dust out.

Fossa – Fossa is pronounced 'foo-sa'. They have long tails, which helps them to balance as they move along the tree branches. They like to hunt alone, except in breeding season, when they move around in hunting parties.

Gorilla – Gorillas have their own unique nose print. They can grasp things with both their hands and their feet. They also have very similar senses to humans, as they can hear, see, smell, taste and touch. Unfortunately, the gorilla is an endangered species.

Hedgehog – Hedgehogs are found in Europe, Africa and Asia and have been introduced into New Zealand. They are nocturnal, which means they mostly come out at night. When they are born, they are blind and also have no quills.

Ibex – Ibex have very special hooves that allow them to climb steep, rocky cliffs without ever slipping or tripping. Each hoof has a sharp edge and underneath they are hollowed out to act like spoons, so they can grip on tight and climb without fear of ever falling.

Jaguar – The jaws of a jaguar are so powerful that they can even pierce a turtle shell. They are carnivores, which means they only eat meat. Jaguars also love to swim and even catch the occasional fish or two.

Koala – Koalas spend most of the day in trees, but when they do come down, they can walk on all fours. They have very sharp claws that assist them in climbing trees. They also have extra thick fur on their bottoms, so they can comfortably rest on branches all day.

Lynx – Lynxes also enjoy swimming and do catch the occasional fish. The tufts of black hair found on their ears are not just there to look good – they actually serve a purpose and work as a hearing aid, adding to the lynx's great hearing ability.

Moose – Mooses are terrified of wolves, as wolves hunt them in packs. The wolves chase them into shallow streams or frozen rivers where they can't move so well. Sometimes wolves bite a moose on its very sensitive nose.

Narwhal – Narwhals' tusks are very long – in fact, they can be up to three metres in length! Narwhals don't do well in captivity at all and those that have been brought into captivity only live for a few months.

Okapi – If you see an okapi with two knobs on the head, you will know it is a male. Males are very protective of their territory but do allow females to pass through to eat. They mark out their territory using scent glands on their feet, which leaves behind a tar-like substance.

Panda – When a panda is born it is smaller than a mouse, but eventually it grows to be about six feet tall. Pandas can also see in colour. When they communicate, they do so with a bleat, a honk or a yowl.

Quoll – This spotted marsupial, the size of a domestic cat, is a predator that eats rats, birds, eggs and rabbits. The tiger quoll develops a pouch only when needed in the breeding season.

Raccoon – A raccoon doesn't hibernate, but it can go into a winter rest. They eat as much as they can in spring and summer, so they can store body fat for the cold winters. Raccoons don't have any real predators, but baby raccoons are afraid of wolves and bobcats.

Skunk – Fortunately skunks don't often use their smelly spray as a weapon. They only have enough spray to use about five or six times and it takes about ten days for the body to make some more, so skunks would rather save their precious foul-smelling spray than waste it.

Tiger – A group of tigers is called a streak. Tigers keep their claws sharp for hunting by pulling their claws back into a protective sheath. They also leave deep scratch marks on trees to mark their territory.

Unicorn – According to popular myth, unicorn horn was believed to neutralize poison. A person afraid of being poisoned would therefore only drink from a cup made of unicorn horn.

Vicuna – Vicunas are grazers and spend all day eating tough mountain grass, which unfortunately wears down their teeth. As a result, their teeth grow all through their lives. They also have extraordinary hearing abilities.

Walrus – Walruses change colour when they go into the water. They become a lighter shade; often they turn almost white. Their whiskers are used for feeling around as they root for food along the ocean bottom.

Xenarthra – Xenarthra is a super 'order' of the anteater, the armadillo and the sloth. Instead of having separate bones in their pelvis they have one solid bone, which is a specially strengthened backbone. Anteaters have no teeth, and sloths and armadillos have no front teeth.

Yak – Yaks live in high altitudes and need extra oxygen to live. For this reason they have big lungs and a big heart. To keep them warm in the very cold months, they have matted hair under their shaggy coats. They also huddle together in the cold, with the calves in the centre to protect them from the blistering wind and snow.

Zebra – Zebras can run one hour after being born. The male zebra is called a stallion and the female is called a mare. Their eyesight is very good and because the eyes are positioned high up on the forehead they have a wide range of sight.

My own recipes

My own recipes